MW00908537

Danny the Dinosaur

written and photographed
by
Mia Coulton

Look at

my dinosaur book.

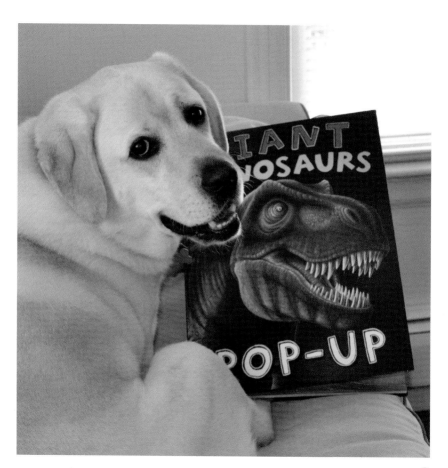

Look at

my dinosaur balloon.

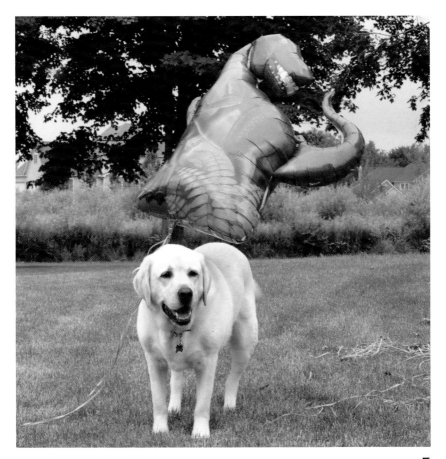

Look at

my toy dinosaurs.

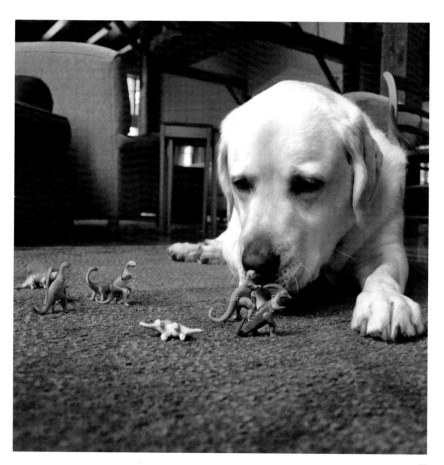

Look at

my dinosaur stickers.

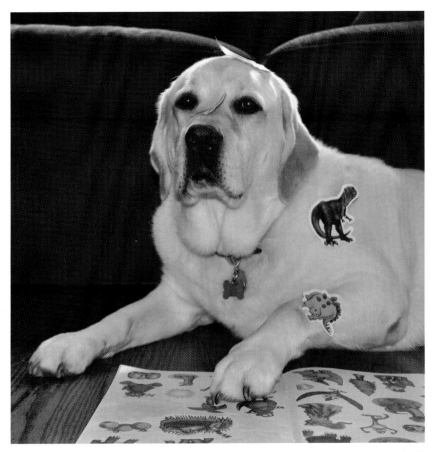

Look at

my dinosaur food.

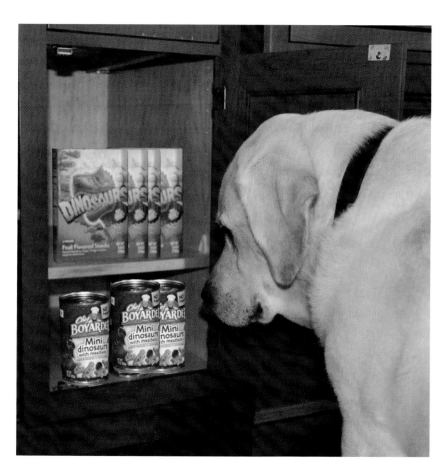

Look at me,

Danny the Dinosaur.

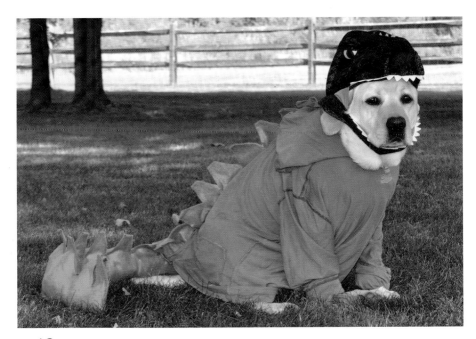